Wrecked: A Blue Collar Bad Boys Book

Blue Collar Bad Boys, Volume 4

Brill Harper

Published by Brill Harper, 2017.

This is a work of fiction. Similarities to real people, places, or events are entirely coincidental.

WRECKED: A BLUE COLLAR BAD BOYS BOOK

First edition. August 4, 2017.

Copyright © 2017 Brill Harper.

ISBN: 979-8223700371

Written by Brill Harper.

About this Book

I knew the moment I saw her bent over the hood of her car on the side of the road that Layna was trouble. It looked like the opening scene from a porno—a shapely blonde in a short skirt waiting for me to tow her sports car out of a ditch and dirty up that sweet, pure body with my filthy mechanic hands. I could hear the *bow-chicka-bow-wow* soundtrack in my head. Then she opened her sassy mouth and everything about my reclusive, sensible, quiet life changed because Layna is not reclusive, sensible, or quiet.

Unfortunately, she's also mine.

We both knew it right away, whether we wanted it or not. But she's got her demons, and I've got my work cut out for me.

She thinks I'm big, surly, and overprotective. She has no idea. Whatever she's running from, I'm going to fix. Whatever she needs, I'm going to give her. And the sooner she figures out what she needs is me, the better off we'll both be.

Author's confession: Like all my Blue Collar Bad Boys, this hero is outrageous, excessive, overblown (heh), and overdone. Just the way we like them. He's dirty; she's sweet. He's from the wrong side of the tracks. She's a poor little rich girl. It's trope heaven up in here. Also, not to spoil anything but there might be neckties and bedposts happening. What would you do if the dude on this cover was *bound* and determined to let you do whatever you wanted to his body?

Chapter One

Layna

I've got ninety-nine problems, and one of them is that I just used my one phone call to ask the tow truck driver I met in a ditch yesterday if he'd be willing to bail me out of jail.

It was the only phone number I could remember off the top of my head because 555-TOWR is kind of lame. I probably told him so at the time, too, but in retrospect, I guess it works as intended. After all, I did remember the dumb phone number.

An hour later, the tow truck driver and I exit the county jail together, and the sunlight is jarring. Like when you get out of a matinee movie and you expect it to be dark but it's still afternoon. But I bet to people already outside, the sight of the Hulk-sized muscle man in greasy coveralls next to the pint-sized sorority sister in an Amour Vert romper is equally discombobulating.

I thrust my hand out to him in goodwill, my jail-issued paper bag clutched close to my body in my other. "Thank you, again, for everything. I'll pay you back." Somehow.

He stares at my hand, then brings his hands to his hips and glares down at me. My tow truck driver, if you remember, is very large, and this pose is intimidating. Or it would be if I were not now a seasoned criminal with a rap sheet.

Okay, he's still intimidating, and I'm probably more "lightly" seasoned than anything. Though sometimes my language is salty.

He's glaring at me, so I pull my hand back. "You mad, bro?"

Why I said that? I don't know. I'm going to blame spending too much time on Greek Row. Or something like that. Because that was over-the-top dumb.

I've never much thought about the word "seething" before, but that is what the tow truck driver is doing. He is *seething* at me. And it makes my heart race a little. A lot. Okay, I'm freaking out now. He is really big but so far just surly in all my dealings with him. But he's the kind of guy whose button you probably can't *un*push once you've set him off into his gamma radioactive rage. Something I now wish I'd considered before calling 555-TOWR. And certainly before I'd asked him *you mad, bro?*

I take a step back, and he takes a step forward. His dark eyebrows slash menacingly above his eyes, his dark beard not hiding the grimace on his face. "Thank you very much? *That's* what you have to say?"

"Would you rather I *didn't* thank you?" I huff indignantly. Because how else does a person huff? "I appreciate you coming to my rescue. Twice in two days. So, thank you for being a friend." I flash my pearly whites. That usually works on men.

"A friend?" He looks to the heavens for support. He doesn't find his answer there, but he does seem to calm after a breath or two. "Do you even know my name, Layna?"

"Yes," I scan his coveralls for the badge I'm hoping is there, "Rogan." He's glaring harder. "Wait, is that your real name? Is it your first or last? What kind of name is Rogan anyway?"

Rogan yanks the paper bag of my belongings away from me. "You're coming with me."

"Um, no. Please give me back my—"

"Look, you have been a pain in my ass for two days, and I'd love to sever all ties with you. But I just paid a bail bond, and if you cut and run, which you are likely to do, then I'm out the money and the reputation I staked on getting you out today. I promised Sheriff Brand you'd be a model citizen. So, until your court appearance, you and I are stuck like glue." He palms my shoulder. "Truck is that way."

I don't really want to bring Rogan into my problems, but it's not like I have anywhere to go just now, so I smile sweetly and head for the tow truck. Maybe he will take me to a diner because...oh my God, am I famished. This town is super small, but they have to have a diner, right?

While we are eating, I will need to figure out my next step. I've never been on the run before. I've never crashed a stolen vehicle before, either. It would all be very exciting if I weren't screwing up my entire life with every ticking minute.

Rogan, or Mr. Rogan, gets in the tow truck after securing me in the passenger side for the second time in two days, and as soon as the door closes, he starts with, "What the fuck is even wrong with you?"

"Excuse me?"

"Do you need a translator?"

"Do you kiss your mother with that mouth?"

"So help me, princess." He does the breathing thing again and wrings the life out of the steering wheel. "Why are you like this?"

Well, there's the question we'd all like an answer to. But I'm not sure his *this* is the same as my *this*. "Be more specific, please."

He hardly even knows me, after all. Our dealings yesterday were not long and involved. It's not like we traded life stories. He towed me out of the ditch. I pretended I was getting ready to pay him, but since I didn't have any way to do that, I took off in the car that didn't really run very well anymore. Well, it ran, but it didn't steer the way it used to pre-ditch, so I ended up wrecking it for the second time on the first corner. Hence the police involvement and my evening in the pokey.

But really, that's not enough information for him to judge me about. I don't really know what he thinks is so wrong with me. And I tell him so.

You know how guys get that weird veiny thing in their forehead? Yeah. He gets that and says, "You stole a car."

"It was my car!"

"Not according to the guy on the title."

The guy on the title is my stepdad, and we're not going to talk about him. "I've been driving that car for three years. It was given to me by my father before he died."

"Where were you going?"

"North."

"North," he repeats.

"Yes. North." That was the extent of my plan. My now derailed plan. My need-a-new plan hasn't shown itself yet, but I hope it is better than the old plan.

"What is north?"

"It's a direction on a compass."

What would happen if that veiny thing exploded? It's looking pretty close. "Have you ever been spanked?"

"Oh my God, pull over and let me out." Why did I not realize getting into a truck with an unknown dude was a bad idea? It's like the first thing my parents probably taught me. Now, I'm trapped with a pervert who's into who knows what.

"Relax, if I ever spanked you, you'd be on board."

"Um, no thanks." I shudder. Oddly, though, I do relax. I am beginning to worry about my state of mind. It's not like me to be so cavalier with my safety. Also, it's not like me to imagine, even for a teeny tiny little second, what it might be like to be bent over some man's knee while he … okay, I need to stop this right now. Obviously, being in jail has poisoned my mind.

"Why north?" he repeats.

"North is further away from home."

I didn't mean for my voice to crack there at the end, but when it does, Rogan's head swings toward me, and I'm subjected to a very long look.

You know what? I'm not the only one acting out of character here. I bet Rogan doesn't bail strange women out every day. "Why did you come to the jail today? We aren't friends. We aren't really acquaintances. And technically, since I didn't pay you yesterday, we're not even in business together." He nods as he's making a left turn, but doesn't answer. "So, why did you come to get me out?"

"Honestly, I don't know. You're trouble. I feel like I walked into the middle of a movie scene and have no idea who the characters are or what the story is about when I'm around you."

I settle into my seat. "I'm pretty sure the movie we are watching is one of those straight-to-video deals with a convoluted plot and really bad actors."

Nothing makes sense. I've been trying for three years to turn my life into something that does. But since my dad died, it's just been one horrible thing after another. At least before today, I thought I understood myself, even when everything around me seemed surreal. But now, sitting next to this stranger, I don't even have a grasp on my own self anymore.

Chapter Two

Rogan

I don't have an answer for Princess Piss-Me-Off. Not really. When she called and asked me to bail her out, I'd like to say I was just curious. But that would be stupid, and I'm not a stupid man. Usually.

Everything about her annoys me and has since I met her. But, oddly, I like her. A lot. And it amuses me that she pushes my buttons so easily. Amusement is a new feeling for me.

I don't get it. I don't like it. I don't want to. But there it is. Something about her spoke to me on a level I don't get to with many people, and I couldn't leave her in that jail cell.

Even if she'd tried to stiff me for helping her. Even if she was some poor little rich girl with an attitude problem. Even if most people in this town would consider me a recluse.

But I'm smart enough not to let her out of my sight now that she's my responsibility. Not if I want that bond money back. Not if I want to make sure I know what happens to her. She's a runner. She's not the first woman in my life to be one.

I turn off the highway, and she looks at me again. I don't even have to see her looking at me to know she's doing it. I *feel* it. Like there is some sort of tether between us. It's kind of fucked up.

"Where are you taking me, anyway?"

"Home."

She inhales sharply. "No. I'm not going back there. I won't. I don't care how nice you've been to me or how much he paid you. You can't make me go back there."

Adrenaline hums through my blood at the tone in her voice. That's fear in there. And I don't like my girl scared. She's feisty and annoying and rubs me all wrong, but that doesn't mean I'll allow anyone to hurt her. "I meant my home. And sometime real soon, you're going to tell me about the asshole that's got you so upset."

I see her shrug in my peripheral vision. "It's nothing you need to worry about."

"Forgive me if I don't believe you."

"Why? Why do you care? You don't even know me."

She's right. I don't. And yet, somehow, I think of her as my obligation.

"I can't explain it. I just do." It's quiet for a minute. Which I imagine doesn't happen often with my little princess. "Why did you call me? Why'd you get into this truck with me? Whatever you're running from must be pretty bad if you've thrown in with me."

"Why do you say that?"

"Well, for one thing, you don't know me. I'm driving you into the woods, and I haven't given you your phone back, yet you're more worried about me taking you home than to a possible serial killer lair."

"I trust you." She twists in her seat to face me, and I risk a quick look at her. "I can't explain it. I just do."

She's pretty. I already knew that. But when she's saying that she trusts me and looking at me with those amber eyes, it strikes me in the chest just how pretty she really is.

I'm sure part of her trust lies in the fact that I'm a good ten years older than her, and she probably sees me as some old guy who helps people on the side of the road for a living.

But I'm not that safe. And I'm not that old.

That feeling in my chest is spreading lower now. She's more than pretty. That sassy attitude doesn't just piss me off, it also gets me off. Or it does now that I'm thinking about it that way.

Shit. I should have left her in that cell. She mighta been better off.

Not sure what I was thinking bringing her home anyway. I haven't had a woman to my house since...well, since my mom took off when I was a teenager. The first three years after she left, I never had anyone over to the dingy trailer we lived in because I was afraid they'd figure out I was living there alone and make me go to foster care. After I turned eighteen, I guess it just never occurred to me to bring outsiders to my place anymore. I have friends, I've had women—I just don't have them over to my house.

Now I'm bringing a stranger home.

We drive in peace for a few miles when she asks, "How far away do you live?"

"A ways. I like my solitude. And my quiet."

"Then why on earth are you bringing *me* there?"

It startles her when I laugh. I'm surprised by the laugh, too. I'm not a man without humor, unlike what I'm sure she believes about me, but there hasn't been much to laugh at today.

We pull off the main road, but it's still two miles to my cabin. Two miles of thinking time. For my part, it's spent on wondering what she's running from.

When I first met her yesterday, I'll admit my first reaction was, "fuck yeah," when I came upon her bent over the hood, her short skirt riding up those biteable thighs. Her ass is extra juicy—round and luscious. She's got long blonde hair like a movie star, and the whole setup looked like the beginning of a porno.

But as soon as she started talking, I realized the situation was more *Blair Witch* than *Tammy Does Tow Trucker*.

Layna speaks in circles. No, Layna speaks in crazy eights. Just when you figure out what the hell she's talking about, you realize she's already changed the subject and you're behind again.

It put me off long enough to purge my indecent thoughts—for all of two minutes. Then my thoughts got worse. Ways to keep that mouth busy topped my brain. Then when she started really speaking her mind, and I realized she was testing me for some reason, thoughts of leaving my handprints on her naked ass kept me uncomfortable in my coveralls.

She'd been trying, yesterday, to see how far she could push me. So the harder she tried to get me to crack, the more control I pushed back at her. Which, for future reference, drove her batshit crazy. She didn't like that I wasn't someone she could manipulate. I have a feeling most men fall over their own feet trying to please her.

So when she was finally out of my hair, and I should have been relieved, I found I missed her mouth, her ass, and even the attitude.

Well, now I've got her. I don't know what I'm going to do with her. But I've got her.

When my cabin finally comes into view, I watch for her reaction. The car I dragged out of the ditch, her clothes, and just her general attitude show she's from money. My cabin is probably smaller than her bathroom. She'll probably make some redneck jokes.

Not sure why I care, though.

"I feel like Laura Ingalls Wilder," she says jumping down from the truck before I can get to her side. "If I call you Pa, will you call me Half-Pint?" she asks as I round the front.

"You call me Daddy, and I'll call you anything you like." Her eyes go round with shock, and I mentally kick myself. I don't even know where that came from.

"You're kind of a dirty old man, aren't you?" She's not scared, just teasing me. It feels like a long time since I've been teased by a pretty girl.

Woman.

I open the front door. "You have no idea."

I'm keeping it light. I'm not that good at flirting. When I want to get laid, I usually make myself pretty clear and that has worked well for me in the past.

Dating has been more miss than hit, but that's on me, too. I'm not a misanthrope—but I am reclusive. The people I like, I like a lot. The rest I don't expend my energy on.

She takes in the front room of my cabin with a huge smile on her face. "There are a lot of books in here."

"I like to read." I've always liked to read. Reading was my escape as a kid and my solace when my mom took off. I could always get lost in a book when real life got too hard. When I had to read by candlelight when the power was cut off. When I spent my first holidays alone because I couldn't tell anyone she was gone.

Now, life is better. I still read, but I spend holidays with friends, and I can pay my power bill.

Layna likes everything about my house but my office loft. "What in the world is happening in here?"

"You've never seen paperwork before, princess?"

"Is this how you run your business?" Her hands go on those curvy hips, and she mimics my pose from the courthouse steps. "How do you track your profitability if all your receipts are in messy piles?"

I lean against the wall and want to chuckle at her incredulous tone. "If money is in the bank, it's profitable. If it's not, it's been a bad month."

"You have got to be kidding me." She starts rifling through my piles. I should stop her. It's not her business what I make or don't make, and she's still in stranger territory. But I don't stop her. I watch her mutter to herself and say mean things about my ancient computer.

"What kind of business software do you use?"

"There's a spreadsheet."

The look she shoots me is almost murderous. "This is a crime scene."

"What do you know about receipts and invoices?" I try to lead her back to the stairs, but she resists.

"My father taught me a lot, actually. I'm good with numbers."

Her voice changes when she talks about her father. She gets this sad, faraway look in her eyes, so I change the subject. "Are you hungry?"

"Famished, actually. I had a dry turkey sandwich hours ago courtesy of the Iron Bar Bistro. Last night I guess, now that I think about it."

"Sounds delicious."

She shrugs. "Almost."

I lead her away from my disaster of an office and to the bathroom. "There's a clean robe on the hook and a towel in the cupboard. I don't have any fancy princess soap, but you can freshen up while I put together something that is hopefully more appetizing than prison food."

"Why are you being so nice to me?"

She's looking less porn-dream right now. Her hair has lost some of its bounce, and the circles under her eyes mean she probably slept like shit in jail. For some reason, though, I don't want to stop looking at her. She's the prettiest thing I think I've ever seen. And I want to wipe away some of that tension and make her feel safe from whatever she's running from.

"Maybe I like you, Layna."

She snorts. "As if."

"I think you deserve a break."

Her eyes well up and she nods her thanks. I turn to leave her in peace, but she grabs my wrist.

"Is it really Rogan?"

"Lance Rogan, but everyone calls me Rogan."

"Thank you, Rogan. I'm not usually so lost."

I let her go without an answer. Truth is, I'm not usually so found.

Chapter Three

Layna

The bathroom is small and very lumber chic, but it's clean, and though it's probably rude to take advantage, the hot water tank seems pretty big.

In lieu of princess soap, I'm left with an invigorating bar of green to use on my face, body, and hair. But squeaky-clean feels lovely. The problem is now that my immediate hygiene is taken care of, my brain has energy for ruminating on my many, many problems.

What am I going to do now?

I have no access to my credit cards or the money in my account. My phone works, but it's probably not safe to use. I've got no wheels. And no friends except for the taciturn tow truck driver who is actually very nice.

I'm pretending I don't think he's nice to look at, too, because that causes a whole slew of other problems I'm not ready to deal with at the moment. Being attracted to a completely inappropriate man is not helpful.

I find some store brand lotion under the sink. Better than nothing. It's goopy at the top like it hasn't been used in a long time. Rogan is low maintenance, it seems. Bless him, though, for the spare toothbrush I find still in its cellophane package.

When I feel human again, I open the bathroom door, and oh my God. Bacon. The man is cooking me bacon.

Now I'm not just attracted to him, I want to marry him.

I follow my nose to the kitchen. "Are you my guardian angel, Mr. Rogan?"

He turns slowly, but where I've come to expect a brooking-no-patience-with-you-look, instead I get a long perusal. A long, intense perusal.

Rogan's eyes darken, and my nipples pinch tightly beneath his robe. *Stop it.*

He breaks the awkwardness first by turning around to tend to the pan. "It's just about ready. Have a seat."

"Can I help with anything?" He's holding himself very rigidly. "No, I got it."

I sit at the bar, and he plates us a meal for a king. Okay, it's eggs, bacon, toast, and juice. But it's the best eggs, bacon, toast, and juice I've ever had.

"Do you want coffee?" he asks after I've made too many indecent moans around my fork.

"Oh my God. I would do anything you ask for a cup of coffee."

Our gazes catch, and my blush is four-alarm, but he moves his eyes to my lips and I sigh.

He gets up quickly, almost knocking over his juice in his haste, and moves across the kitchen to start a pot of coffee.

"So, you live here alone? Is there a girlfriend who isn't going to be pleased that you're harboring a known felon here today?"

He doesn't turn around but shakes his head. "No girlfriend."

I like watching the way he moves around his space. It doesn't seem like he should be so graceful. His muscles bunch under his thin t-shirt, and I'm a little too captivated. His arms are covered in colorful tattoo sleeves, something I hadn't noticed earlier as they been under coveralls or a flannel shirt. He's also absolutely ripped. Like maybe he bench presses the cars after he pulls them out of ditches.

"You seem like a catch, Rogan. Why no lady friend?"

The color of his face darkens when he looks at me, and I think that it's a blush, which tickles me to no end. "I think we both know I'm not a catch. Most women want a man who talks."

"You talk."

He holds up the sugar bowl, which I decline. "Not much. Not with new people anyway."

"*I'm* new people. You talk to me just fine." I take the cup he offers and doctor it with creamer. "Lots of women like quiet guys. Then we don't have to fight for the spotlight."

"You don't feel like new people."

I've got the coffee mug to my lips, but I pause there as his words connect inside my brain. He's blinking at me like he can't believe he said that either.

"You don't feel like new people, either," I admit and then take a drink. The guy may skimp on bathroom products, but his coffee beans are top quality. "I know you don't usually bring your tow truck rescues home. I really appreciate everything you've done for me."

He takes the stool next to me again, his presence warm and safe. I haven't really felt safe in a while, I guess. Not since my dad died.

But even as I feel safe, there's an undercurrent of energy that isn't about safety. A zing I've never felt before. And I wonder if Rogan feels it, too.

"You seem like a very capable woman, Layna, but something tells me you're in over your head. I'd like to help you."

The clouds in my coffee don't offer me much in the way of answers, but I continue to stare into the cup. I don't feel capable. Not at all. But I don't think I can share my burden with Rogan. He might try to help, and that's the last thing he needs to do. The guy my stepdad owes money to is bad news. It's better that Rogan just thinks I'm a flighty mess than try to step in and get involved. I'd never forgive myself if he got in too deep trying to save me. And he would.

I twirl my hair and pretend my life is the way it was a few years ago. The old Layna. "I'm just your average spoiled princess running away from her princess problems, nothing for you to worry about."

"You could go to jail for the car."

I shrug and finish the coffee, setting the mug down like I'd just done a shot. "I'm sure I can just buy my way out of it, right?"

He's up and spinning my stool around until I'm caged between the mass of his body and the counter now behind me. "Wrong answer."

My heart rises in my throat. He's so masculine it's insane. A girl could climb him like a tree. A Testosterone Tree. "You don't need to worry about me. I'll be fine. I always bounce back better than ever."

My voice cracks on *ever,* and he furrows his brow. "Talk."

"And say what? What do you want to hear? I'm spoiled and a pain in the ass. I'm reaping what I've sown. Poor little rich girl."

He's staring at my mouth, and my pulse kicks up. "I think that's what you want me to believe. But you're hiding something."

"I'm not your problem, Rogan."

"You don't trust me."

At the moment, I don't trust myself. He smells delicious and those hard muscles beneath his shirt make promises about what he's capable of. The strength he possesses. I bet a girl in his arms wouldn't be afraid of anything ever again.

But that's not for me, unfortunately.

"I don't trust anyone." Not anymore. Not since my dad died and my mom brought Alan into our lives. Not since she died shortly after that. "It was nice of you to cook for me. I'll do the dishes."

There's a moment between us. He's still too close; it's too intimate. But somehow, he's not close enough.

"You need to trust someone."

If he would look away from my eyes, I might be able to think. Maybe.

"You're in my house." He says it like that makes sense.

"Yes, Captain Obvious."

The tic in his jaw is a work of art. "You're wearing my robe." He moves his head so we'd be cheek to cheek if we were an inch closer, and he inhales. "You *smell* like me." He pulls back and all that broody focus is trained on my eyes now. "That means you're mine. You can trust me."

Chapter Four

Rogan

It's evening now, and I'm wondering why I backed off her in the kitchen earlier. It wasn't what I wanted to do. I wanted to take her, right there, right then. Truth is, I wanted to mark her. Claim her. Keep her.

But it wasn't right. She's got demons she's running from, and I'm not a man who takes advantage of someone. She might need me, but she doesn't need me pawing at her like a beast until she trusts me.

She looks so small in my robe right now, curled into the corner of the couch and reading. If I didn't know better, I'd say she's fragile. But she's got a spine of steel.

I recognize the haunted look in her eyes. She's not the spoiled brat she shows the rest of the world. Well, she's definitely a brat, but spoiled I'm not so sure of.

She's got rich girl background, but her life is harder than she lets on. Or it used to be. Until she met me.

Now she's not alone. I let that sink in. At first, it feels heavy, and then suddenly light and warm. The second I let go of the resistance to wanting her, I feel free. There's no reason to fight it. It can't be stopped.

New feelings inside me settle bone deep, and things clear up the way the sun eats the fog.

She's mine. Mine to protect. Mine to take care of. And it maybe seems too soon, but I think she's mine to love.

I never thought I'd feel this way. I've seen other guys fall. I've read books and seen movies, but I never believed it was something I was capable of. Life with my mom had never been easy, but after she abandoned me altogether, I'd pretty much put my heart in deep freeze.

Until my annoying princess drove her Porsche Cayman GTS into a ditch. Shame, too. It was a really nice car.

Damn. It sure as hell doesn't make any sense. She's ten years younger than me. College educated. Used to guys in sports cars with trust funds. And I want to throttle her nearly as often as I want to kiss her.

I didn't even know her before yesterday. I should try to rationalize this away. Explain it. Make sense of it.

It's not logical, I guess. It's love.

I get up and boil some water for tea. The storm outside is getting worse. That usually means I'll get a call tonight. I already don't want to leave her. What if she needs me? What if she takes off?

"Whatcha doing in there?" She's sitting up on her knees looking over at me from the back of the couch. Someday, I'm going to bend her over that couch. Someday when she trusts me. When she knows me. When she loves me back.

"Making you tea. I'm hoping it will knock you out so you don't take off in the middle of the night if I get a roadside assistance call."

"You make tea?" She wrinkles her brow like she's trying to figure out an algebra problem in her head. "You going to roofie it?"

"The thought crossed my mind." I pull a mug down. "I'd rather just trust you."

"I'd rather you didn't."

That's strange. I tilt my head. "Why don't you want me to trust you?"

"I don't want to disappoint you."

She's lost too much. It's painted all over her face. Whatever forced her "north" is going to answer to me someday. "You aren't going to disappoint me."

She shrugs and turns back around, opening her book and leaving me with more questions than insight again. I wish I understood her better.

I wish she'd let me in. But as a well-known recluse, I understand her barriers.

I'm just handing her the tea when the pager goes off.

"You have a beeper? That's very...retro."

"It's issued by the roadside assistance company." I make the call, get the details, and give my guest the once-over. "Lines are down all over the place. I don't have to explain to you how dangerous it would be for you to take off on your own tonight, do I?"

Layna raises one eyebrow at me, and it's sexy as hell. "I don't really want to wander around the woods at night during a storm. I left my hiking boots in the trunk of the Porsche."

"Do you even own hiking boots?"

"No, not really."

"I don't want you to go, Layna. It's dangerous out there. You don't know the terrain, and bad things could happen to you before I even knew you were gone." She opens her mouth to argue, but I interrupt her interruption. "I can't keep you here if you don't want to stay. I want you to *want* to stay." I point to the hooks near the door where all my keys are hanging. "If you run, don't go on foot. Steal my car. It's in the left bay of the garage outside. Keys are on the wall and marked."

Her eyes get real big. "You are giving me the keys to my escape?"

"No, I'm showing you where they are and hoping you don't use them. I'm hoping you'll be passed out and snoring when I get back, safe in bed and drooling on my pillow. But if you need to endanger yourself, I'd rather have you endangered in a vehicle than on foot."

"I kinda thought you would just tie me up or something."

"You wish."

She blushes, and I want to pull open my robe and see how low that blush goes. Instead, I kiss her forehead. "Stay."

HOURS LATER, WET, TIRED, and grumpy, I open the cabin door and find Layna sound asleep on my couch. I exhale the breath I'd been holding since I left her.

She's still safe.

I'm drawn to her like she's reeling me in on her fishing line. I lean down and press another kiss to her forehead.

As I pull back, she blinks her eyes open. She frowns for a second as she comes to, then she throws her arms around my neck. "You're home."

She's sleep-warmed and perfect, so soft and lovely. And then she's kissing me.

I don't think either of us expected it.

Her lips are amazing. I try just sipping at her sweetness, but I want more. I need her softness, so I clutch her hard and she swings into me like we've been kissing for years instead of barely knowing each other. She angles her head, and I deepen the kiss. I want in her mouth, in her body.

She pulls back, confused I think. Maybe she was sleep-kissing, but I don't think so.

"You're soaking wet," she says. She's not accusing me of accosting her in her sleep. That's a good sign.

"Yeah. Raining. Outside." This girl has made complete sentences a challenge.

She bites her lip which I find adorable. I'm not usually a guy who uses the word *adorable*. "I should be ashamed of myself. I totally just attacked you, didn't I?"

"Yeah. You want to do it again?"

She nods and tightens her hold on me as she dives back in for another kiss. She's petite enough that, with little effort, I pick her up and settle us back onto the couch with her on my lap.

I'm trying to keep this light. Keep us in this sweet spot to savor, but with each pass, my hands grasp her tighter, my mouth pushes harder. I'm feeling my heartbeat in my cock when she opens her mouth and moans as my tongue accepts her invitation inside.

Her fingers tunnel through my hair, and she rocks her hips, grinding us together. The robe is gaping in the front, and I catch glimpses of the perfect curve of her tits and I'm lost. I can't stop my hand as it reaches in to palm one breast while my other grasps the back of her neck and holds her still so I can fucking plunder her mouth.

Her skin is so smooth beneath my callused hand. I feel like a hulking beast let loose in a store of fine, expensive china. I don't want to hurt her or scare her. I'm sure her college boys don't maul her so roughly, but when I pinch her nipple she throws her head back and lets out the hottest sound I've ever heard.

With her neck arched that way, I take advantage and kiss my way down. She's beautiful in her abandon. I don't deserve this stolen moment, but I take it. I ravish her unblemished skin, marking it red with my beard and my teeth.

"Oh my God," she cries.

As much as I love her neck, I want back in her mouth. I suck her tongue, and then I thrust mine into her like I'm fucking her.

Like I'm going to fuck her.

She's like holding fire, her flames hot and bright. Her passion consumes me, and I burn with a lust I've never felt before.

I push the robe off her shoulder, exposing her breasts to me. "You're beautiful." I pull back enough to get her in a better position to suck that sweet tit in my mouth.

That's when I notice the bruises.

Chapter Five

Layna

Nobody has ever made me feel like this before. I've never been able to just let go, lose myself. I'm not even sure how we got here.

I fell asleep worrying about him out in the storm, and when I woke up and he was right there, so handsome and so close, I gave in to my instincts.

Turns out my instincts rock.

"Who did this to you?" he asks.

"Huh?" I'm mad that he's pulled me out of my fantasy and back into my head. "Did what?"

He presses the lightest of kisses to my arm where angry purple bruises have formed.

Damn.

"It's not important."

Oh, Broody McBrooderson's gaze gets all dark and intense. "The fuck it's not."

Mood broken, I pull the robe back on and cover myself. This is not a conversation I want to have, much less have while exposed.

"Dude, you are harshing my mellow."

"Don't do that."

"Do what?"

"When you are trying to distract me, you pull out your college-girl airhead routine because you know it annoys me."

"I am a college girl." I push him back so I can get up. "All I have to do is breathe to annoy you anyway."

"Who fucking put his hands on you?"

Ignore. Distract. "I didn't want to dig around your dresser while you weren't here, but I was hoping you maybe had some more clothes I could borrow. This robe is..."

"Is it who you're running from? Is that why you don't want to go home?"

"Just a t-shirt and maybe some boxers would be fine."

"Someone grabbed you hard enough to leave finger-sized bruises on your arm. Tell me his name, and I will cut off his hand."

I gasp at his sudden propensity for violence. Despite his size and his grumpy attitude, Rogan has been a gentle giant in my presence. "It's nothing for you to worry about."

We stare at each other for too long, him trying to pierce my brain and get my secrets, me trying to build a wall. The less he knows, the better.

"I'm sorry I kissed you." *I'm not.*

That makes him blink. And then he gets this look that is equal parts disappointed and hurt. So he gets up.

"Rogan—"

He holds his hand up to stop me and silently walks away. I cover my face with my hands. God, why do I screw up everything? A normal woman could probably have turned that whole thing around and had him inside her by now. Instead, I'm alone again.

I feel the weight of his hand on my leg, and I uncover my face. He's on his knees on the floor in front of me. His eyes are the richest shade of brown and full of concern I don't deserve. "Rogan, I'm—"

"You're not alone anymore." He picks up my hand. It's so small inside his. "I know you don't trust that yet. And I shouldn't get frustrated with you. It's going to take time. But you'll see. You'll look back someday and see how every memory we share from here on out is me not letting you down, and then you'll believe. I can be patient."

I'm stunned. I don't know what to say or think or feel. I can't process what he's saying, it's too much. But the feeling of not having to face everything alone for once…I don't even realize I'm crying until he wipes a tear so gently off my cheek. Thunder rumbles in the distance.

"Why don't you want to go home, Layna?"

"My stepdad."

"What did he do to you?"

"It's not what you think."

"Then tell me."

Maybe it's worse than he thinks.

"My mom met Alan after my dad died three years ago. I pretty much thought he was a sleazeball, but she really liked him." I shrug. "He was always nice to her. Really nice. So I guess I just thought maybe any guy that wasn't my dad was a sleazeball and I tried to get along with him. For a while anyway."

"You were close with your dad?"

I nod. "Very. He was my hero." A pang of longing pierces my heart, doubling me over. God, I wish Daddy were still here. He'd have known the right thing to do. He always did the right thing.

But then, if he hadn't died, I wouldn't be in this mess, either.

Rogan is still on his knees on the floor in front of me, watching me so closely.

"Alan lost all my dad's money pretty quickly. I think he used the bulk of it right away to get himself out of debt. I still have some set aside in a trust fund, I think, unless he found a way to access it. But I can't get to it until I'm twenty-five. People started coming to the house. Taking things away. My mom…she didn't handle it well. First losing my dad and then losing her wealth. She was kind of fragile."

"Was?"

My whole body gets cold. "She started taking pills. Alan found her this strange doctor who got her whatever she wanted whether she needed it or not. And about a year ago, she was gone, too."

"Gone?"

"She died. Overdose." My hands are trembling, so he takes them in his, giving me comfort. It's been a long time since I've felt comfort. "I blame Alan. I wanted her in rehab, but he just kept bringing that stupid doctor around until I was an orphan."

I was sad when she died, but it was hard to mourn the shell of the person she'd become. My mother, the woman I loved, had been dying since the day she met Alan.

"Alan managed to get everything that my father owned into his name by then. Everything except for my trust fund. We had a fight. He knew I thought he was a loser, and he hated that. He was a real macho man, didn't like that I didn't fall at his feet. At some point, he found my journal. At first, I didn't know it, but I realized later he'd been using it to sabotage me. He figured out all my weak spots. He screwed up my grades, got my friends to alienate me." At Rogan's questioning look, I explain, "He used my passwords I had written down to mess with my college assignments and grades. He used my social media accounts to mess with my friendships. My phone. He was whacked out like *Gossip Girl* on steroids."

"I don't know who *Gossip Girl* is."

"Well, I'll never believe *Gossip Girl* is Dan, but that's another story. It was a TV show. And we're getting way off track. Anyway, Alan ruined me from the inside out. And then he read an entry and found out I was a virgin."

Rogan stiffens.

"He sort of sold me to one of his 'business associates.'"

"He what?" Rogan explodes.

"He set up some sort of date with some old guy he owed money to. I figured out at that point what was going on. How he knew so much about me. How he'd turned everyone against me. The buyer was coming into town a few weeks later, so I made a fake entry in my journal. About the night I snuck out and lost my virginity. I came home from school and Alan was there. Livid. Shaking. This strange angry red color." I shiver. I've never seen anyone so close to a psychotic episode. "He ranted and raved at me for an hour and then decided I made it up. He called that doctor, the one who turned my mom into a vegetable, and locked me in his office until he could get there."

I rub my arm where the bruises are tender. "I didn't go willingly, as you might imagine."

"Why did he call the doctor? Was he going to drug you?"

I shake my head. "I don't think so. The doctor was there to...he was going to have him examine me. For a hymen."

Rogan loses all color in his face. "Fucking Christ, he's a dead man."

"So, while I was in his office, I hacked his computer, tried to move a little money around, tried to access my trust, but couldn't. And then I found the keys to my car. The one he'd been keeping from me for the last week, forcing me to be a prisoner in my own home."

"You escaped."

"I escaped."

Rogan's big hand, so gentle yet capable of so much, cups my cheek. "You're the strongest, bravest person I know."

Which of course sets me off into tears.

"He'll never hurt you again. I promise. You are not alone."

I've been so alone for so long, I'm not even sure how to feel. Grateful seems like a tame word. But I also feel responsible. I don't want Rogan dredged into my crazy world. He's got this great, quiet life of no drama, and I just come barreling through like the Kool-Aid man going through a wall.

"He isolated you for too long. You're like a flower that needs sun."

A dandelion maybe.

Rogan fixes my robe. I'd forgotten I've been sitting there with my boobs out. *Nice one, Layna.* "Well, at least now I understand what was north," he says.

"What was north?" I ask. Because I have no idea what I was heading to other than away.

"Me."

Chapter Six

Rogan

She's not sure of me yet. And that is fine. I can be patient. I need her to choose me anyway. She's been manipulated enough.

"We can tackle all this tomorrow. You need to sleep."

"No comments on my virginity?"

"Not tonight."

"I'll sleep here on the couch."

I shake my head. "You take my bed, princess." I want her in my sheets. I want my pillow to smell like her.

She looks at my couch dubiously. "I can't do that. You've done enough for me. I'll be out of your hair tomorrow."

I hope she can see in my eyes that will not be happening. But I don't want to scare her. "I won't ever lock you up. Not like he did. I swear."

"I know that."

"But you're stuck with me."

She doesn't look scared. But she does look sad. "Rogan, I think the guy he sold my virginity to is some kind of mob man. I can't bring you into this."

"I'm already in this."

"If anything happened to you because of me..."

"Do I look like I'm afraid?"

She shakes her head. "I don't think you're afraid of anything."

"That's not true. I'm afraid you won't trust me to help you. I'm afraid you're going north again the minute I let my guard down." God help me if she does.

"You can't possibly be this altruistic. And if it's just sex you want, I can't believe there aren't a lot easier ways for you to get it. Why are you so eager to jump into my problems and help me? A normal person would wish me well and send me away."

"First of all, I'm not doing this to get in your pants."

She shrugs.

"Darlin', if I were just after getting my dick wet, we both know you wouldn't be a virgin anymore." Those amber eyes get all wide and round, then narrow into slits. Before she can let her spitfire attitude rise to the top, I go on, "Yeah, I said it. And I'll say worse and what's more, you're going to like it. I'm a filthy sonofabitch." She's just blinking rapidly, and I can't believe I've found her mute button. I file that away for later. "You were rubbing on my dick earlier, and we both know it wouldn't have taken much to convince you to ride it all the way. It's more than sex between us, and you know that, too. It has been since the minute you opened that sassy mouth. Maybe we don't make sense to the rest of the world, but I'm not worried about them right now. I'm only worried about you. So, yeah, we're gonna fuck. But not yet and that's not what's keeping us here."

"Okay, caveman. What makes you think you're going to be the one to take my virginity?"

"I'm not taking. You're going to give it to me. When you're ready. Nobody makes that decision but you." I stand and pull her up. "I'm going to steal your fucking heart, though. You can be damned sure about that."

She rolls her eyes. "You're awfully cocky. Where do you get all that confidence from?" She holds up one hand. "And don't go for the easy joke about being cocky, please." I raise my eyebrows. "I know exactly how much you're packing." She blushes, and we both remember her grinding on my cock not that long ago. "But, seriously. You met me yesterday, and I'm a hot mess of daddy issues and a felon now besides. Why on earth are you interested in pursuing this?"

I take that hand she's holding up and kiss the palm before placing it over my heart. "I have no fucking idea."

She snorts and then starts laughing and it's the best sound. Well, I guess I like all her sounds. But her laughter is easily in the top five.

"C'mon, princess. You need a good night's sleep."

"They're going to be looking for me. My stepdad is going to know I couldn't get far when he comes to retrieve his stolen car. And I don't know how much the guy paid for my...if he can't get the money back from Alan, he's going to come for me."

"That's a tomorrow problem." I lead her to my bed and pull the covers back before turning to the dresser to get her the requested t-shirt and boxers.

"What's a tonight problem, then?" she asks, twirling her fingers in a gesture, so I turn around while she dresses. Fuck, knowing she's bare is killing me.

"Tonight's problem is how I'm going to sleep with this cock as hard as iron knowing you're in my bed."

"You can turn around."

Layna is in my bed, the sheets up around her chin. It's almost perfect. Since I won't be getting in it with her, it's not quite. But I like her in my bed. A lot.

"You have such a dirty mouth, Rogan. I feel like I should be clutching my pearls around you."

My mind immediately goes to giving her a pearl necklace. Of course.

"I like making you blush, princess. I'm going to say a whole lot worse, I promise. Good thing you like dirty talk."

"How do I know what I like? I'm a virgin, remember?"

My cock is like a steel pipe in my pants right now. Fuck. A virgin. I'm going to be the first and last lover she ever has.

But not tonight.

"You were grinding on my cock like a girl who knows what she likes. We're going to be really good together."

But not tonight.

I kiss her forehead. Again. I like the way it makes me feel, though. I like treating her tender. I'm gonna like treating her rough, too.

"Goodnight, sweetheart."

She grabs my arm. "Wait. We could share the bed. I think I could roll over two or three times without getting to the other side. There's plenty of room."

My cock aches. "I don't think that's a great idea."

She bites her lip again, but this time it's not adorable. She's scared. "Please stay with me."

How could I say no? "Okay, but no hanky-panky. I don't want to wake up to find you jumping me while I'm asleep."

"Did you just say hanky-panky? Like for real?"

I just smile and grab some sweats to sleep in, changing in the bathroom. It's going to be a long fucking night, knowing she's so close but I can't touch her.

Not yet.

Chapter Seven

Layna

I've been living with Rogan for a few days now. We've been in this weird holding pattern. Like pleasant roommates most of the time until he looks at me a certain way, his eyes all dark, and I get instantly wet. Like, gushing wet. It's not normal. It can't be.

I've never felt like this before. Never been so aroused and wanting. And I think he can tell.

If I were here against my will, I would say I have Stockholm syndrome. The way he touches me softly when he passes by me. The way he looks into my eyes when I'm talking, like he's really listening to what I have to say. I'm falling for him a little more with each passing hour. Trusting him. Wanting him the way I should not.

I am currently wearing clothes he bought for me at Walmart. Eating food he bought for me because I have no money. I am contributing very little to the cause, and I hate it. Which explains why I am currently stirring a pot of chili that doesn't...look right.

I excel at microwave food. The rest not so much. But I wanted to do something. To try to show my appreciation. Chili sounded easy.

Chili lies.

The sound of tires on gravel stops my heart until I look out and see the familiar shape of Rogan climbing down from his truck.

I meet him at the door. "Come with me." I grab his hand.

"Hello?" he says as I drag him over to the loft stairs.

"Don't be mad, okay?"

"What did you do, Layna?"

"I was bored. You leave me alone for really long periods of time, Rogan." I take a deep breath and continue so he won't. "And don't say something sensible like *I have to go to work*. I get that. I do. But I want to contribute. So, don't be mad."

"What is that smell?"

I take a whiff. "Chili."

"You made chili in my office?"

"Don't be ridiculous. I made chili in your kitchen. I did this in your office." I lead him to his now clear desk.

"Where is all my stuff?"

I roll my eyes. "I filed it, dummy. You can't run an efficient business if you don't know where anything is."

"I don't know where anything is now. You moved it all."

I open a file cabinet. "There are these amazing things called files. You can put paper in them after you input the information to an ancient spreadsheet."

"You did my bookkeeping for me?"

"I know I overstepped. And I'm sorry not sorry about it. It's just that you have been doing all these things for me and I've done exactly nothing in return and I'm good at business and finances so I thought—"

He stops me with a kiss. "Thank you."

"Thank you?"

"I hate bookkeeping."

"I couldn't tell." I get another kiss. "So, you're not mad?"

"I'm not mad—" The smoke alarm interrupts him with a horrible scream.

"Shit. That's probably the chili."

We rush downstairs into the smoky kitchen. Nothing is on fire, thankfully, but the soup pot is scorched and dinner not salvageable.

He doesn't get mad about that either. I mean, he's not like jumping for joy or anything. But he's so even-tempered. After the last three years of Alan and his rollercoaster of emotions, I forgot what it's like to be around a man who can control his temper. I mean, even at his most aggravated, all Rogan has done is frown strongly at me.

I get that tingly feeling way down low again when I look at him waving a towel frantically below the still screeching smoke detector. He stops the movement, staring back at me. "What?"

My feet are moving, propelling me toward him, and I jump, knowing he'll catch me. He does, his hands planted on my ass, my legs wrapped around his middle.

"Burnt chili turn you on, little girl?" he asks before my mouth crashes into his. I like the way his body is hard against all my soft places. I like the way he walks us into a wall while he devours me. "Fuck. You taste so good."

He pushes into me, his cock hard already. Which gives me a hollow ache where his penis should be. I think he's hard enough to push through all our clothes and my hymen, too. I'm going to lose my virginity against a wall fully clothed. I writhe on him, feeling pretty good about the impending orgasm his hard cock is about to give me.

I shout when the stars come, throwing my head back and hitting my head on the wall behind me. Rogan grunts his pleasure. "You're amazing. I love watching you come."

The world spins and I'm on the couch. We're pulling each other's shirts off, desperate for more skin. I can't get enough of him. I lay down, pulling him on top of me. Rogan's hard chest is a heavy weight. Pushing me down while he's pulling up feelings and sensations that are new, yet instinctual. I want with so much longing, yet a sudden shaft of ice replaces my spine, and I freeze up like one of the bad motors in his garage.

I don't say stop, but Rogan is in tune with my body enough to feel the change. Hell, maybe my body feels as cold on the outside as it does on the inside.

He pulls back. "What is it, wildcat?"

I clench my jaw. "Nothing." I don't know. Why don't I know? Why can't I let go?

His brow furrows angrily, and I recoil. Oh God, I've finally pushed his last button, haven't I? Who could blame him? I brace myself for the yelling. If he's anything like Alan, there is sure to be spittle also.

"Easy, Layna, easy." He rolls off me gently, pulls me up, patting me. "I'd never hurt you."

"You're mad. I've made you mad."

Raw shock changes his expression. "No, angel. I'm not mad at you. Never at you. I'm frustrated that you're keeping something from me. Something is wrong. I can't make it better if you don't tell me what it is. I'm mad that someone made you feel like you can't be honest. That someone made you scared that if my mood darkens, it's your fault or that I would ever take it out on you."

"You have every right to be mad that I led you on this far and then pulled back."

"Layna, look at me." I don't want to. I want to put on more clothes. All the clothes I can find would be nice. I need to cover everything that's exposed. I don't want it out there. But I can feel the weight of his stare on me, imploring me to give him what he needs from me. So I look.

"I'm a man. A real man. I don't take something that isn't freely given. I don't expect things as due to me somehow. If you aren't ready to lay with me, I'll wait. That's what real men do. I might try my best to soften you up so you get ready. But I would never be mad at you for needing more time."

He is a real man. Not like Alan. He's patient and protective. He's virile and masculine, but always in control of himself. Of the situation. He's safe. I know it deep inside, but I'm still wary.

"Rogan, you make me really want to be ready. I want you. I really do. I'm not even sure what stopped me. I'm sorry that I'm so messed up in my head. I've just felt trapped for so long that I'm afraid of giving you the last bit of control or something."

"You've had to protect yourself for too long. And that man tried to break you, but he never did. And he never will. You're strong, sweetness. You can trust yourself."

My heart is cracking in a million places right now. This gentle giant next to me could do anything he wants to me, but what he wants is for me to freely give myself. "I don't know how to get over this feeling. If I ever will. I kind of want you just to overpower me and take me. You know, hump me past the hump."

He takes my small hand in his over-sized paw. "Someday, we'll do that. I'll fuck myself into you and you'll take it. You'll beg for more. But not yet."

A rush of moisture spreads through my core at his rough, sexy words. But he's holding my hand so gently, and his tone is so even. Like I'm a scared stray he's trying to take in for my own good.

"What if I'm never there? What if I'm permanently damaged?"

"You're not."

"What if I am?"

"I have an idea."

He pulls me up to my feet and leads me to his bedroom. He opens his dresser and pulls out a few neckties. My heart inches up my throat.

I go for humor first. "When was the last time you wore a necktie? Why do you even have neckties?"

He laughs. "I haven't worn these. Every year Mabel Hartley, the salon owner, gives me a tie for my birthday. I think it started when she was hoping I'd court her daughter."

Yeah, okay, the little flash of red that covers my vision is cliché, but that's what it feels like. I've never been jealous before. "Oh really?"

"Relax, wildcat. Her daughter and I never dated and she's long since married. But Mabel still gives me a tie for my birthday. I have a drawer of them."

I'm coming down from my irrational anger, but coasting right back into my irrational fear about what he plans to do with the neckties. "I don't know about this idea of yours. I think tying me up might make it worse." Surely, he won't try to convince me otherwise. I can't even swallow.

"They are not for you."

Oh. *Oohhh.* "Wait, you want me to tie *you* up?"

He steps into my space. This mountain of a man with no shirt, barefoot, and the top button of his jeans undone. Holy fuck, that is hot. My muscles loosen and I inhale deeply. Then he hands me the neckties.

"I'm going to lay on the bed, wildcat. And you are going to tie my wrists to the bedposts."

"And then?"

"And then anything you want. I am at your mercy. You can touch me anywhere. Do anything you want. Or nothing at all. It's all up to you."

"Are you serious right now? I feel like you just gave me a plate and pointed me to the buffet at the Bellagio. Anything?"

"Anything."

He's giving me his trust. Can I give him mine? "What if...what if I want to stop? You won't get mad?"

"This is all for you. All about you. It's not my buffet." He leans down, his breath next to my ear causing the little hairs on the back of my neck to stand up. "Someday soon, you're going to be my buffet. And I'm a hungry, hungry man. When you're ready, I plan to feast on you for hours." He stands up straight as my knees are turning to jelly. "When you're ready."

"Hours?"

"Has anyone ever eaten your pussy?"

God, you'd think I'd be used to his dirty words already. But no. He says pussy and mine quivers. "No. Nobody has ever...touched me there."

"Say pussy for me."

I shake my head, the blush heating my cheeks. "I can't."

His warm eyes have crinkles in the corners when he smirks at me. When a gargantuan man has warm eyes with crinkles, a girl starts losing her inhibitions. "You're a felon who's done time in jail. You can say pussy."

I bite my lip, and he grunts. The kind of grunt that cavemen might use. I want to hear it again. "No one has ever touched my pussy." I like the way his eyes darken. "No one but me, anyway."

He grunts again and I feel powerful. "Oh fuck, baby. That's hot...you touching yourself. You better tie me up now."

He hands me the ties, but I don't know how to do this. "I'm not exactly well-versed in knots."

Rogan makes some complicated loopy things and puts them on the bedposts. Then he lays down in the middle of the bed. "Come here and tighten these up."

I want to look at him first. He's massive, sprawled like a man with no worries. Even giving me control of his current destiny doesn't take that ease from his features. I want that. I want to just be able to rest and know that life is going to be just fine. And the first step in doing that is right in front of me.

Tonight, I can just be.

I crawl up the bed and straddle him, enjoying the surprise lighting his eyes. I lean over and tighten the ties, noting his eyes are on my face, watching me. Gauging me to make sure I'm okay.

I'm more than okay.

I lean back on my haunches, resting on his rock-hard stomach.

"Anything I want?"

"My body is yours."

Mine. His body is mine. I can do anything, explore anywhere. I have control here. I start with his scalp, running my fingers through his thick, dark hair. It's soft, silky. I know it's not the kind of intimate you think of when there's a man tied to your bed, but touching him tenderly, massaging his head, is actually making me tear up a little. It feels so good to be close to someone. Who am I kidding? To him. It unlocks something inside me when his eyes drift closed and he practically purrs.

I trace my fingers lightly across his ears, through his scratchy beard, over his heavy brow. His eyes open when I smooth over his lips.

"Go ahead. Learn every inch of me. Know me."

I nod and palm over his burly shoulders slowly, feeling the hard muscles beneath his smooth skin. I can't wrap my hands around his biceps. I think the man can tow cars out of ditches with just his arms.

Slowly, I slip my hands down his forearms, the wiry hair is soft, but not soft like his head. He's so solid. I'm in awe of the way he can get through life without breaking anything he touches.

His hands are rough, of course. But clean. He takes care of them as well as his tools, I suppose. I pick one up and linger over the lines of his palm.

"Am I going too slow?" I don't want him to be bored.

"You're going just perfect."

I don't know about that, but I am having a good time learning him. Knowing him.

I come back up his arms, over his shoulders, and press against his chest. The hair on his pecs crinkles, and when I pass gently over his nipples, his body tightens beneath me.

I can feel the banked power in his body. His legs are not tied down—he could probably still do whatever he wanted to me. But he holds himself in check while it looks like he's holding down an electric wire.

So I tease circles around his nipples, getting close but not touching, and he groans.

Oh, I like this.

I grab my hair to one side over my shoulder and lean over him, using the ends of my mane to tickle his chest.

He moans again.

"Like that, do you?"

"Fuuuuck."

I think I am beginning to feel drunk with power. I tease more, using my hair along the sides of his torso until he starts shaking.

I zero in on one nipple and draw it into my mouth, sucking and biting while his arms strain against the ties.

I'm bolder now. Kissing and licking all over his chest and moving down. There's a lot of skin here. He's so wide and firm. The texture of his skin changes. I dip my tongue into the grooves of his six-pack, lost in the sensation.

"You're killing me and I love it," he moans.

"I love it, too, Rogan."

He looks to the ceiling, reminding me of the day at the courthouse. No help for him up there. He's the one who keeps inviting this trouble into his life.

The lower I go, the more I feel the bulge in his pants pressing into me. Yeah, he's big there, too. Of course, he is.

"My goodness, Rogan. Your pants must be hurting you."

He sighs hard. But he won't insist I take them off.

I climb off him and pull the zipper down, giving him relief. "You should have said something."

He grunts. Silly man. I pull them down, past his hips, and then completely off. He's still got his boxer briefs on, but they are tented up.

I'm not quite ready for that yet, so I start my exploring at his feet and work my way up.

When I reach for the waistband of his briefs, he asks me to stop. "You don't have to. I don't want you to think you've gone past the point of no return if you aren't ready. We can stop. Anytime."

"If you think I'm leaving without this prize tonight, you're delusional. I don't want to stop." To make my point, I yank the briefs up and over his straining cock, pulling them down his legs.

It's fucking huge. I have serious doubts that thing will even fit inside my body. But my mouth is watering and something very primal insists on my next move.

I touch my first penis.

It's powerful, strong like the rest of him. He's velvety, a surprise I guess. But so far, everywhere I've touched him is a different texture, each oddly pleasing to me. Like he was somehow formed for my pleasure.

But this cock.

His eyes are squeezed closed, and his entire body is tense as my fingers skate up and down the shaft. The mushroom tip is weeping pre-come, and I use some of it to make the slide of my hands easier on us both.

Rogan starts mumbling gibberish. Mostly filthy words that turn me on even more, especially knowing they are being ripped out of him.

I push his legs wider so I have more room. I hold his cock up and rub my cheek along it, making friends. Worshiping it.

"Rogan?"

The tendons in his neck are tight. "Yeah?" he croaks.

"I love your cock."

"Oh fuck, baby. You're going to make me come."

"I hope so."

I run my tongue around his tip, noting where he gets more sensitive, savoring the flavor of him. I give him little licks, like a kitten lapping milk, and his hips are thrusting up and down like he can't control himself.

I don't want him to control himself.

"Can I still do anything I want?" I ask, coyly.

"Fuck, you can have the title to my fucking house. Yeah, do whatever you want. It all feels good."

"Good," I murmur, nuzzling the place where his shaft meets his balls. He smells to me the way fresh sheets feel. Clean, comforting, warm.

"What I want is to take you in my mouth. I want you to come in my mouth. Can we do that?"

I don't wait, just suck him in as far as I can get him. He feels amazing on my tongue, in my mouth. The weight of him, the scent of him, the taste of him. I can't stop one hand from reaching into my pants to rub my clit.

And that is when he finally loses that control.

"Oh fuck, baby. Yeah, touch your clit while I pour into your mouth."

The first spurt goes all the way to the back of my throat, and I almost gag, but that's okay. There's more.

His body is wracked with shakes and he comes and comes, cursing me in between telling me he loves me. He's completely gone, and I took him there. That's when I come against my own hand.

Chapter Eight

Rogan

I'm sure I'm dead. I have to be. No man can come that hard and live to tell.

My arms are killing me. Pulling against the ties has been a resistance workout I'm not used to. Jesus.

My girl is still half clothed, resting her cheek on my leg. I want to pull her closer. I need to touch her, but this is her show, not mine. I can't complain. I'm fucking sated.

"I'm still a virgin," she mumbles against my leg.

"Yep."

She lifts her pretty face to look at me. "That was amazing."

"Yep."

"Is that all you have to say to me? Yep?"

"Nobody has ever made me feel an orgasm with my entire body before. You are the most amazing woman I've ever met, and I think I can smell colors now."

She grins. "That's better." She comes up the bed and begins loosening the ties. "Your body is like a fun park, Rogan."

I shake out my arms. "So, you are okay? You liked what we did? I feel like maybe I got all the fun and you got all the work."

She lays her head on my chest. "I loved what we just did. I loved everything about it. I am a huge fan of your cock."

"My cock worships you, princess."

"Good. Does that mean you'll make me something to eat then? You'd think I'd be full right now, but..."

"I'll make you anything you want. And you can still have the title to my house."

Layna giggles and it's the best sound ever. "I wasn't sure you'd remember that promise. You were a little out of your head when you offered it."

She doesn't get it yet. That anything I have is hers. Time will tell. I kiss her forehead and go to the kitchen to make my woman a snack.

I wasn't sure the tying me up thing was my best idea. It was an instinct—I wanted to give her control. I wanted her to get past that fear that kept stopping her. I didn't realize I was going to love it so damn much. Her hands and her mouth on me was heaven. It was more than sex. Has to be. I've never felt anything like that before.

And now I'm getting hard again. Alfuckingready.

I almost drop the plate of sandwiches when I get back to our bed. I'd expected her to be snoozing, or maybe thinking. But she is sitting up, under the sheet, and her pants are on the floor.

Yeah, my dick is for sure getting harder now. She's naked in my bed.

She raises one eyebrow the way I love.

"I can't tell if you are hungrier for this sandwich or my dick right now."

"Sandwich first, dick next."

"Seriously?"

She nods. "Yeah." Reaching for her food before I even sit, she tells me, "I'm an addict now."

"Happy to be your supplier."

We eat, but the tension between us is growing stronger. I fucking want that pussy. Bad. But I need to make sure she's not just going along with things in order to not be a virgin. Or in order to please me because she thinks it's expected of her.

She nudges me. "You get a crinkle between your eyebrows when you're thinking hard."

"Yeah. I just want to make sure you're completely on board."

"Rogan, the reason I took my pants off was because they were completely soaked since I was so wet. I'm on board. One-hundred percent. I want you inside me."

I'm not any kind of superhero. That is fucking enough for me. I want inside her. I want to claim her. And yeah, if that makes me some kind of caveman because I want to be the first one in, I don't care. I'll be the last one in, too. She's never going to need another man because I will give her whatever she wants. Whatever she needs. I'm whipped and I don't care. Not one fucking bit.

She pulls the blanket off her body, and I get my first look at her naked.

"You're perfect." I lay on top of her, wanting to feel all of her against my skin. She's so soft. Round. My cock is between us, insistent, but it will have to wait. It had its turn and will get another. But now it's time I get to know her body. I move down slowly, drinking in the scent of her skin, that taste of her.

She lets her head fall back when I nuzzle at her mound. After I place an almost chaste kiss there, I say, "I'd rather you watch me." She lifts her head and questions me with a look. "I want you to watch me. I want you to watch me turn you inside out."

I lick her slowly, making eye contact with her. Using my fingers to separate her pussy lips, I use my whole mouth on her. She moans, struggling to keep her eyes on me like I asked. "You taste so good, baby."

My beard is scraping her inner thighs. I want to eat her out until my jaw locks up. Until we pass out. I don't think I'll ever get enough of her. "Your pussy is so wet, Layna." I plunge my tongue into her, and her hips arch off the bed. "Anybody ever make you come like this before?"

"This again?" She shakes her head. "Rogan, you're the only one who's ever touched my pussy. You're the only one who's ever tasted me."

I reach up and grab one tit while my mouth gorges on her gorgeous cunt. *Only one. Only one. Only one.* Her sweet body is taut like a livewire beneath me, tense and vibrating. Her fingers pull my hair and then she pushes my head into her like I'm trying to get away. I'm probably squeezing that tit too hard, but she starts crying out my name as she comes, so I guess she's doing okay.

Hell, she's more than okay judging by the amount of cream on my tongue. I haven't even gotten my fingers in her yet. I need to. She's tight and I'm big. I don't want to hurt her. But I can't wait to plunge my fucking cock into her.

I rest my head on her stomach, giving us both a break for a second. She's still got her fingers in my hair, and like earlier, she's massaging gently. "I want to stay in this bed with you forever, Layna."

I rub my bearded chin across her tummy a couple times, making her giggle. Someday, when I rest my head there, she'll be full and round with my baby. The thought of it sends a shock of heat through my blood. Fuck. I want to come inside her so bad. "Someday, I'm putting a baby in here."

Let her be shocked. I'll never be anything but honest with her.

"Oh, Rogan. Why is that so hot?"

"Because I'm your man. I'm yours and you're mine. Someday—I know not now, but someday, I'm going to knock you the fuck up."

She giggles again. "You're such a caveman. *Me breed Layna. Make baby.*" She stops laughing. "Oh my God. That really is hot. I'm not even joking. Tell me again."

I sit up and bend her legs, plopping my cock on her mound and tapping it against her clit. "I'm going to fucking breed you, Layna. I'm going to come in you so hard and so often and with so much come, you'll be leaking me out for days."

"Yes, yes. Oh shit, I love it when you talk dirty."

I slide my dick between her slippery folds, and we both hiss with pleasure. I fit the tip in enough to notch us together. "I don't know how much longer I can last. If you have any second thoughts, now is the time, princess."

She reaches between us and rubs my shaft, holding me against her succulent pussy. "No second thoughts. I want you."

I want to go in bare, but I pull out.

"Where are you...what are you doing?"

"Condom."

Layna raises to her elbows. "I had my Depo shot last month. And...well...I didn't realize when I was cleaning your desk you'd also have so many personal papers. I filed your medical papers, too. I'm sorry...I tried not to look, but I saw you get tested regularly."

I suppose I should be mad that she invaded my privacy, but I don't care since I'm about to invade her pussy. "Depo shot?"

"Birth control. It lasts three months." She gets pink. I had my tongue inside her pussy not five minutes ago, but she's blushing about birth control. "We don't...if you don't want to...I'm safe. You're safe."

I don't know how it's possible, but my dick just got even harder. "Are you saying you don't want me to put a condom on?"

She is every fantasy I've ever had. Mouthy, sexy, smart, and now I get to fuck her raw? If I last two strokes, it will be a miracle.

"I don't want anything between us." She eases back down and reaches for me. "I want to feel you. I want to feel it when you come inside me."

I'm leaning over her and my arms are shaking because it's taking every damn ounce of strength I have not to slam into her, take that cherry, and spray her with my come. "Anything you want, princess."

I start with one finger. She's wet, but she's so tight. I add a second while I put a little pressure on the pearl of her clit. She tenses for a second, then releases a breath. I'm working her open, loosening her, but I feel her getting nervous. I relax and keep my fingers still while I move up and kiss her. She opens her mouth and I slide my tongue in, distracting her while I pull out my fingers and get my cock in position.

My tongue in her mouth and my cock in her pussy is the best moment of my entire life. I ease in a little more and meet the resistance that makes me pause.

"Don't stop."

"I don't want to hurt you."

She wraps her legs around me, digging her feet into my ass. "Don't stop."

I thrust hard, and my girl cries out. I hold still, let her adjust, pray she doesn't hate me or ask me to stop. Christ, the walls of her pussy are squeezing my cock so tight. It's heaven and hell at the same time. I need to take. To claim. But she needs me to be in control just a few minutes more. "I'm sorry, baby. Breathe, okay?"

She takes a deep breath. "Talk dirty some more?"

That's my girl.

"I'm going to fuck you full of come, Layna. And you're going to come so hard around my cock. Your sweet little pussy is going to worship this cock." I ease out and back in, slowly, evenly. "And after, when you're a quivering, come-covered puddle of girl, I'm going to go into the kitchen and make you another sandwich."

Her eyes open and she huffs out a laugh. "Yeah, you fucking are."

"You ready, baby?"

She nods, I can see the pulse in her throat hammering. "Yeah. I'm ready."

I pick up my pace. A little harder, a little faster. And then I look down to where we are joined, and I can't stop the beast inside me any longer. I slam into her, a deep thrust that has my balls slapping her ass and her fingernails digging into my shoulders. I pound into her, ramming every inch of my cock into her tight channel. The way she stretches around me, taking it all, makes me even crazier with lust. Then she stiffens.

"I'm coming. Oh, Rogan, I'm coming!"

Her cunt starts squeezing, milking me, and I can't stop myself from following her over the cliff. One last, brutal thrust has me holding her down and pouring into her. "Take it, baby. Take all of it."

I come for a long time, the aftereffects continuing as my cock keeps spurting. I am wrung out and shaking, but so is my girl, so I roll onto my back and pull her with me, my dick still buried inside her. I'm about to doze off after the best sex I've ever had when she taps my shoulder.

My eyes open.

She grins. "If you'd be so kind as to go make me a sandwich now?"

"You're a sassy girl. But since I promised you a sandwich..."

"And your house."

"And my house."

"Rogan?" she asks as I'm halfway across the room.

"Yeah, babe?"

"After the sandwich, I want you to come in my mouth again."

Chapter Nine

Layna

Tires crunching gravel never used to scare me so much. But Rogan is already home. Rogan is also a recluse and nobody else ever comes here, so it's unusual. *Please don't be bad news.*

I head downstairs from where I'd been working on installing QuickBooks onto a computer that is probably too old to take it. It was a miracle that he agreed to the software—I'm not optimistic about my chances of getting him to buy a whole new machine.

"Stay here," he tells me. Like I'm his pet dog. He gestures to the loft.

"I don't think so."

He growls at me. "Layna."

"If it's trouble, and we both know it is going to be, you're not handling it for me. I won't let you."

Rogan curses under his breath and puts a shotgun behind the door. I didn't even know there was a shotgun in this house. I stare at it, trying to still my heart. Shit is getting real and I don't want him shooting anybody or getting shot for me.

Two very large men in black suits are climbing the porch steps. Rogan opens the door and stands in the entryway, his arms crossed over his expansive chest. The dudes in suits are big, but Rogan is bigger.

Fat lot of good that will do if they shoot him, though.

"Mr. Rogan, right? Lance Rogan?" The one with the dark buzz cut asks. The one with the salt-and-pepper buzz cut catches me looking out the curtain.

I'm not exactly trained in subterfuge, okay?

"She's here," he tells his partner.

"Mr. Rogan, we need to talk to Layna."

"Layna who?"

"I just saw her in the window," the other guy says.

"That's my girlfriend. I don't know anyone named Layna."

The men give each other a long look.

"She's not in any danger, sir."

"It'd be best if both of you left my property. You asked about someone. She's not here. Time to go."

One reaches into his breast pocket, so I run out. "Wait, wait, wait. No need for that. I'm Layna. I'll come with you willingly if you promise to leave him alone. Please don't shoot him. Please."

Rogan catches me with one arm around my waist and pushes me behind him just as Dark Buzz pulls out an ID badge.

"Nobody is here to shoot anyone. Layna, we aren't here to take you away. We just need to ask you a few questions."

Oh.

Rogan looks at his badge, then asks for the other man's, too. I try to read it over his shoulder, but I'd need a step-stool. "They seem authentic, baby. What do you want to do? I can send them away, or you can let them talk. Up to you."

I'm sure it's been happening over the last week, but this is the moment I finish falling in love with Rogan. It seems strange that it isn't when he's kissing me or when we're intimate. It's when he gives me room to make my own decisions. He's there for me, I know. He won't leave my side. But he won't smother me or expect me to do what he thinks is best.

"What kind of questions?" I ask.

"Well, for starters, did you know your stepfather is dead?"

YOU PROBABLY THINK I'm too cool to faint like some southern belle in too tight a corset, but you'd be wrong.

The world gets dark, and then the dark gets fuzzy. I remember sliding to the floor, but I don't remember hitting it.

I'm on the couch now. I'm awake but haven't opened my eyes.

"Smooth, Venich." I hear one of them say. "I thought we agreed that you weren't going to shock people like that anymore."

"Mr. Rogan," the other says. "I apologize.

Rogan is stroking my hair. "There are washcloths in the bathroom. A cold, wet one would be good right now."

I guess I should admit to being conscious. I blink slowly, and Rogan is staring at me, concern etched into every feature.

"Hey," I say, for lack of better sentiment.

"Hey," he replies.

"Sometimes, I'm such a girl."

Relief loosens up those lines a little. "I usually like it very much when you're a girl. Not fond of the fainting though."

"I'll keep it in mind."

"Want to try sitting up?"

I nod and he eases me up when Salty Buzz comes back and hands me a washcloth. I hold it to my forehead. Breathe a few times. "Is Alan really dead?"

Salty Buzz steps back so Dark Buzz can take over. "Yeah, we're pretty sure it was a mob hit. His body was found in the bay."

Oh, God. I hated Alan, but I didn't want him dead. "Mob?"

It hits me then that said mob might still be after their collateral. Me.

It's time to go north again.

I try to stand, but Rogan holds me in place. "Let the blood settle, sweetheart. You've just had a shock."

"What if they come after me next? Rogan, I won't put you in danger." I plead with Dark Buzz, "Alan promised my...me...to one of them. I don't know who. They might come looking for me."

"That was me you were promised to," says Salty Buzz.

Rogan leaps from the couch and almost lands a punch before Dark Buzz can grab him. "Jesus, Venich. You're the worst at talking," his partner says.

"I was *posing* as mob," Salt Buzz explains to me, quickly, as Rogan shrugs off Dark B. "We've been watching Alan for a while. Working undercover. When he offered your...you...to me, we realized we could add some charges. But then you disappeared before we could conclude the sting."

"Agent Venich was not the only bad guy your stepfather was dealing with, though. His gambling debts caught up with him before we could intervene." Dark B. shoots Salty B. a look to shut him up when he inhales like he is about to speak. "The government has seized all of your stepfather's property. I'm very sorry, Layna, as I know that must seem very unfair to you. We understand it belonged to your parents and should have gone to you, but Alan made sure everything but your trust was in his name. We had the warrant and the property when he disappeared shortly after you did."

"It's all gone?"

He nods.

It's not like I could ever live in that house again. Not after all that has happened, but everything Daddy worked for can't just be gone.

"Your trust is safe. When you turn twenty-five, you get it all. He was unable to touch it."

That means the next four years, I'm on my own.

"We've looked into some things on your behalf. Your tuition for fall had been prepaid, so you can still go to school."

I nod. There's more. Dark Buzz keeps talking, and I pretend I'm hearing, but really, I go into some weird zone. When he starts sounding like Charlie Brown's teacher, Rogan asks him to stop talking.

"Are you okay?" he asks.

I shrug. "Sure."

"Layna, is there someplace we can take you?"

"Take me?"

He eyes Rogan. "You're not on the run any longer. If you'd rather go somewhere else. Somewhere safer?"

"Safer?"

"If you don't want to stay here, or if Mr. Rogan isn't interested in continuing to have a house guest..."

"Layna owns the title to this house. She can stay as long as she likes."

I laugh. It sounds weird. Like a crazy person. But this is his big chance to pass me off as someone else's problem. "Are you sure? I can go...somewhere else."

Rogan's face turns white. "If you want to go, you can."

"What does that mean? Do you want me to want to go?"

"What?"

Salty Buzz starts pacing. "The two of you are dense."

"Venich." Dark B. is holding onto the bridge of his nose. That man is going to have heart problems if he doesn't do something about his blood pressure or get his partner under control.

"I know I'm not supposed to talk, but they are obviously unable to manage this themselves. Look, kids, I'm convinced that Layna isn't being held here under duress. You're obviously boinking, so—"

"Venich!"

"There's no danger. Nobody needs to hide. Nobody is getting whacked by the mob. Nobody but Alan, anyway."

"Venich!"

"So tell him you want to stay. And you," he points to Rogan, "tell her you want her to stay. I'd like to get back to the city before nightfall."

"I want you to stay."

"I want to stay," we say at the same time.

Salty is headed to the door already, but Dark B. leaves us some instructions for who to call to get my personal effects like clothes and how to claim something that is mine that might have been impounded.

They're gone in a whirlwind. Rogan brings me tea again and hands me some paperwork.

"What is this?"

"I started the title transfer yesterday. You need to sign it in front of a notary."

I look down. "Rogan, why are you signing away your house to me?"

Chapter Ten

Rogan

"**I** told you I was going to sign the title over to you. I don't understand why you are so surprised that I did. Have I given you any indication that I am not a man of my word?"

I realize that it might be considered rash, but I was more grateful than ever that I had started the paperwork before we got the news today that she had lost her fortune.

"Rogan, sex talk is not to be taken literally. I understand that and I've only just been indoctrinated this week."

"I know it's nothing like the house you lost, but—"

"Stop. That's not what this is about."

"Then what is this about? I wanted to make sure you had something in your name."

"It's your home. You've worked so hard for it."

"It's mine and I want you to have it. It's not necessary to kick me out, though I suppose that will always be an option for you."

"You're a high-functioning adult. I don't understand why you don't see how this is bizarre behavior. People don't just give everything they worked for to a girl they've been, as Agent Venich so eloquently puts it, boinking for a week. Also, it makes me feel like a prostitute."

My blood pressure rises. "That's the first stupid thing I've ever heard you say. I'm not paying you for sex. I'm giving you something important to me because I love you. When we get married, I'll get half of it back anyway, so it's really not as big a deal as you think."

"Married?"

"Yes, married. I love you. I fully intend to fill you with babies, another thing that was not just sex talk. I'm not saying we do it now, but yeah, when the time is right, we'll get married."

"You're insane." She puts down her tea and gets up to pace. "We've known each other a week. I am a pretty big mess and have been since you met me. I need to get my shit together, and until I do, I have nothing to offer you."

"That's the second stupid thing I've heard you say. Do you think you have to have it together to deserve to be loved? Princess, most of the people on this planet are a mess. None of us know what we are doing. You do your best each day and hope it's working. Then you find the person who makes you feel like you at least understand why you've been trying. I own a business. I work hard. I get up each day and try to be a decent guy. But I don't have my shit together any more than you do, and I've had more practice. I'm surly and reclusive, and I don't need a headshrinker to tell me it's because I never got over being abandoned by my mother. But then I met you and now I understand why I get up each morning. Why I try to be decent. Why I work hard."

She's stopped walking around the room and is just staring at me now, her amber eyes wet. "I feel like I'm in a Julia Roberts movie right now...and no...not the one where she's a prostitute."

"That might be the only Julia Roberts movie I've seen."

She gives me a watery laugh. "I love you, too. I do. But I can't just take all your stuff. I need to figure out what I'm doing. How I can give back? It's not fair to you to take me on in this state."

"You do whatever you need to do, princess. Your house and your man will be right here waiting for you when you're ready for us."

"Rogan..."

"No decisions have to be made right this minute. You have another month until college starts again. I'm not pushing you under or pulling you out of the water, Layna. We can just tread right here for now. Okay?"

"Okay. I think."

"You've got a lot to think about with your stepdad and all. Do you want to go for a walk or something?"

"Or something sounds nice."

My hard-on is instant. I want back in that pussy, and that is a fact. In fact, since she ran between me and the agents on the porch, I've felt a deep need to be balls deep in her again.

I grab her around the middle, fast and hard, enjoying her surprised gasp. Enjoying it even more when I push her roughly over the back of my couch.

"What are you—?"

With one hand planted on her back to hold her down, I yank down her shorts and panties. "Now that I have your attention, Princess Piss-Me-Off, I'd like to bring up the incident on the porch where you ran between me and what might have been a gun."

She twists around, so I restrain her arms. "Rogan—"

"You scared about ten years off my life."

"I'm sorry, but—" She shuts up the minute I bury my face in her pussy.

"Mmmm," I say against her sweet, candied cunt before I snake my tongue inside her as far as I can. She moans and I widen her stance so I can get my whole face involved. I bring her to a hard, ruthless climax, holding her down and not caring how her legs are trembling as I use my feet to kick her legs wider.

"I need to punish you really good for that."

"Punish me?"

I take my dick out. "Never scare me like that again."

"Well, you don't ever tell me 'stay' like I'm a dog again."

I smack her ass like I've been wanting to do since that first day. She shrieks and squirms, but thrusts her ass toward me more.

"Oh baby, the taste of you made my dick so hard. I'm leaking pre-come like a faucet." I tap her lower back with my cock. "I hope you are ready for this. I don't think I can be gentle."

"Fuck me, Rogan," she says. "Fuck me hard. I want it. I want to feel you."

I've still got her arms restrained when I slam into her. We both moan. She's wet, so fucking wet. And her tightness is gripping me, pulling my dick inside her.

I think about how scared I was that something could have happened to her on that porch, and I slam into her again. Harder.

I punish us both with the brutal fucking. The sound of our flesh slapping fills the room. It's obscene and it makes me go at her more. I'm holding her too tight, but I can't loosen my grip. I can't think of anything past the mind-numbing fuck I'm delivering. I should pull back. I should let go of her arms. Touch her clit. I never meant to be so rough with her.

"Oh God, Rogan." Her body is tense and straining.

"You going to come around my cock? You're so fucking wet. Tell me you don't love this. Tell me you don't like being fucked rough and hard. That you aren't dying for my cock whenever it's not inside you."

"Oh God, oh God."

"Tell me who this pussy belongs to."

"My pussy belongs to you, Rogan. Only you."

"Fucking straight."

My balls tighten and my muscles tense, and I drive into her as hard as I can. Just as I'm about to go, her inner muscles clench around my cock and she starts milking my dick.

"Just like that. Such a good girl."

The roar that precedes my orgasm is epic, and I pull her hair and yank her head back as I fill her up like we're animals.

Chapter Eleven

Layna

Five months later

I've got ninety-nine problems. No seriously. This fucking accounting assignment is fucking huge and fucking killing me.

Okay, and I'm a little grumpy.

What kind of sadist assigns ninety-nine accounting problems?

And it's my night to cook. Shit.

I hope my roommate likes sandwiches. Again. It's always sandwich night on my night to cook. Which is why I only have one night assigned to me, yet never manage more than bread. Sometimes, I toast it. That's as far as my culinary skills have progressed.

I could probably distract my roommate by flashing him my boobs. Men are easy that way. But that wouldn't be right, would it? Even though I'm *dying* for some D, I shouldn't use sex to manipulate someone or get out of chores. That's not exactly A+ adulting.

Take it easy. I'm just playing. My roommate likes to be manipulated. I'm still living with Rogan. As if I would flash my boobs to anyone else.

While my tuition for the semester was paid, room and board was not. I was able to transfer to online classes for the semester and stay in the cabin of love with the reclusive tow truck driver. Since I own the house, it made sense to stay where I didn't need to pay rent. And get D whenever I'm dying for it. Win-win.

I never actually signed the title transfer. It's still in a file in the office. But in Rogan's heart, I own his house. It's cute and weird, but whatever.

I have a job now, too. After I convinced Rogan to buy a better computer (by flashing my tits and telling him it would make my schoolwork easier since my classes were online) I began taking on some bookkeeping for some other small businesses in town, with excellent references from my employer. I use the opportunity to give them advice on how to better their businesses, which most of them ignore, but at least they are more organized. I haven't steered anyone wrong yet, and once Mabel Hartley added a manicure station to her hair salon per my urging, she made enough profit to take that anniversary cruise she'd been wishing for with Mr. Hartley.

The people of this town are leaving too much money on the table. I have ideas. I've even told Rogan I'm considering running for mayor in a few years. Give me time, another few years and my MBA, and I'll have this town wrapped around my finger and making profitable quarters.

I thought I would miss university life more, but after the number Alan pulled on me last semester, I'm content to walk away from friends who couldn't wait to talk shit behind my back and shun me before they even talked to me about what was obviously strange behavior. Small-town life suits me better, even though the gossip machine runs much faster than the college one. It's a different kind of gossip, I guess.

And for a self-proclaimed recluse, Rogan has a lot of friends. They were wary of me first—the whole being arrested for grand theft auto thing—but they came around when they saw how happy Rogan is with me. And how I intend to keep him that way.

When Rogan comes home, he's sweaty and gross, but he's still more appealing than these ninety-nine problems, so I join him in the shower five minutes after he gets in it. His face registers shock, and then pleasure as I slide to my knees.

I love all the things Rogan does to me with his cock, but I have a special place in my heart for taking him in my mouth. I like the control. I like making him lose control. And I love the silky weight of him in my mouth. I swirl my tongue around the head of him, over and over. Then gulp him down to the back of my throat.

He groans, a sound I like a lot. "Not so fast, sweetheart." He pulls my face off him, his dick plopping out of my mouth. "Stop pouting and stand up."

"But I want—"

"I know what you want, angel."

My back is against the shower tile, my feet off the floor, before I realize what's going on. At my entrance, Rogan's long, thick cock is waiting. He fills me slowly, stretching me, until he's fully seated. I close my eyes. "I love the way you feel inside me."

His grip on me tightens. "I don't know how I lived all these years without you to look forward to." I open my eyes, find him staring at me intensely. He pulls nearly all the way out, then pumps into me hard. "I love you so much, princess." He takes my mouth in a punishing kiss, demanding surrender, and I give it gladly.

He can have anything he wants of me. He's pinning me against the tile as his thrusts go deeper, harder. Our moans echo off the tiles. He feels so good; everything feels so good. I'm riding him pretty hard, despite having little control in this position.

"You're going to make me come, Layna," he says like a curse. "My little horny princess wants my come, doesn't she?"

I use my fingernails on the back of his shoulders to get better leverage. "I can't wait."

"You're so greedy. Greedy for my cock. Greedy for my come."

His words touch that place in my brain that turns off everything but wanting to breed like animals. It's like he actually pulls a lever inside me that makes me numb to anything but my base instincts. No logic in the world can overwhelm my desire for him to fill me up right now. "Give me a baby, Rogan. God, you..."

"What, sweetheart?" he asks and slows his pumping hips, teasing me and making me crazier. "Finish your sentence."

"You turn me into such a slut. I can't think when you're inside me."

"That's what I like to hear. You can be my slut, baby. You just come and get this cock whenever you need it. My horny little slut." He keeps the slow pace and I think I might kill him. The graceful glide is electric, but I want a pounding fuck now. I try to egg him on with a bite to his ear, but he only laughs.

"Rogan," I groan, trying to angle my hips.

"Easy, sweetheart. There's no rush."

"Please. I need...I need..."

"I'm going to give you everything you need. You know I will." He slams hard, thrusting all the way in and then holds still. "I always give my girl what she needs." He slams into me again and then holds still again. "I know your pussy craves my cock. I can feel all that cream you make just for me. It's all over my dick how much you want me."

"Please," I moan. I need to come. I need him to come.

"You didn't get that shot this month. Every time we fuck, we get closer to making a baby. Is that what you want?"

"Yes!" I cry out. I want it so much. It will likely be months before I can get pregnant, my doctor told me.

He's holding me still again. "You make me feel fucking feral." He buries his face in my neck and nibbles on my neck. In a surprise move, he bites me while he thrusts again. "Need to mark you."

"Do it." I'm on sensory overload. The stinging bites on my neck, the stretching of my pussy, the deep need for him to come inside me—all of it was making me crazy.

"You have the sweetest, tightest, most perfect pussy." He's tense all over, his corded muscles bulging. "Tell me what you need," he orders.

"I just need you. Only you."

"I'm about to give you more than you can handle." He's thrusting in and out now, plunging into me in hard, deep motions. But he stops again. "Marry me."

"What? Rogan, please fuck me—"

"Marry me. Please."

Time stops. I can't hear the water from the shower, I can't see past his warm eyes. The whole world has stopped turning for this one moment. *All he wants is me*, a voice inside tells me. I've been stubbornly holding out on the wedding front. I don't know why. I want to marry him. He says he wants to marry me. I'm just afraid that I've sort of forced him into this domestic relationship with all my drama, and I want him to be sure he never regrets me.

He's shown me nothing but love and care. He makes me laugh. He makes me feel safe. And somehow, I fill a space inside him, too. It's a miracle, and I'd be a fool to ever let it get away from me.

I'm a lot of things, but a fool is not one.

"I'll marry you."

He smiles. "Say it again."

"I'll marry you. I love you. I vow to be your biggest pain in the ass until the end of time. I'm yours. Always."

He squeezes me as he kisses me deep, and though he's not thrusting, we're standing still, I start coming on his cock, squeezing his cock inside me until he follows. We sort of melt to the shower floor on legs on longer able to hold us up, but we're still kissing.

"Say it again."

"The water is getting cold."

"Say it," he warns.

"I'll marry you."

"That's my girl."

He reaches up to turn the water off. I pretty much crawl out of the shower and grab our towels. "So, about dinner..."

"We're having sandwiches again, aren't we?"

I flash my pearly whites—since flashing my boobs is already being done. "Sorry. You're the one who wants to marry a woman with zero skills in the kitchen."

"I like sandwiches."

"I like you, Lance Rogan."

And I do. I love him, of course, but I also like him very much. I was sure I would never make myself vulnerable, not after watching my mom lose herself so completely to grief that she let Alan into our lives.

But this man—this burly, gigantic, hulky man—gives me more than love. He gives me courage. And, if I'm not mistaken, he's going to make me a sandwich even though it's my night to cook.

That's true love, folks.

I hope you loved these two as much as I did. If you're tired of reading about billionaires, maybe you're ready for some real men. Dirty, hardworking, and good with their hands are the kind of heroes you'll find in the *Blue Collar Bad Boy Series*. These guys aren't cultured. They are hot *AF* alpha heroes who know how to take care of the slightly nerdy women they fall for. For reals, this series is more fun than you knew you were missing. And they don't need to be read in order.

So which blue collar bad boy will you choose next? They are all rough, raw, and surprisingly sweet.

Like...the roadhouse bouncer and the actuarial sciences student in *Bounced*[1].

Or...the carpenter and the Jeopardy! nerd in *Nailed*[2].

Perhaps...the oil rigger and the kindergarten teacher in *Drilled*[3].

Mayhap...the tow truck driver and the sorority uptown girl in *Wrecked*[4].

Surely...the brick layer hot single dad and the babysitter in *Laid*[5].

How about...a returning military hero and the wallflower at Christmas in *Tagged*[6]?

Or...the farmer who needs a wife and wants the curvy waitress in *Plowed*[7]?

Or...the hot rancher trying to convince the city girl to stay in *Bucked*[8]?

Maybe...the bomb squad cop and his pregnant neighbor? Did I mention she's a virgin? You read that right. Try *Banged*[9].

1.　　　https://books2read.com/Bounced

2.　　　https://books2read.com/Nailed

3.　　　https://books2read.com/Drilled

4.　　　https://books2read.com/wrecked

5.　　　https://books2read.com/laid

6.　　　https://books2read.com/tagged

7.　　　https://books2read.com/plowed

8.　　　https://books2read.com/bucked

And surely...the modern day Viking bartender and the bookworm virgin in *Tapped*[10]?

---

9. *https://books2read.com/banged*

10. *https://books2read.com/Tapped-A-Blue-Collar-Bad-Boy-Book*

Also by Brill Harper

Blue Collar Bad Boys
Bounced: A Blue Collar Bad Boys Book
Nailed: A Blue Collar Bad Boys Book
Drilled: A Blue Collar Bad Boys Book
Wrecked: A Blue Collar Bad Boys Book
Laid: A Blue Collar Bad Boys Book
Tagged: A Blue Collar Bad Boys Christmas
Plowed: A Blue Collar Bad Boys Book
Bucked: A Blue Collar Bad Boys Book
Banged: A Blue Collar Bad Boys Book
Tapped: A Blue Collar Bad Boy Book

It's Complicated
All Together
All at Once

Love in Brazen Bay
Wrong Number Text
The Right Stuff
So Wrong It's Right

Don't Get Me Wrong

Standalone
Dirty Jobs: a Blue Collar Bad Boys Collection
Notch on His Bedpost
Honeymoon With The Prince:: A Modern Day Fairy Tale
Good Girl

Watch for more at https://brillharper.com.